DISNEY's DUCK TALES

Webby Saves the Day

Book Club Edition

Random House 🏠 New York

Donald Duck was away on a trip.
Huey, Dewey, and Louie went to stay
with their uncle Scrooge McDuck.
A few days after Donald left,
the boys wrote him a long letter.

The boys wrote:

Dear Uncle Donald,
We hope you are having a fun trip! As soon as we said good-bye to you, our adventures began...

The letter told how
Scrooge's helicopter had nearly
landed on them all at the dock!

The pilot was
Launchpad McQuack, of course!
He picked up Scrooge and the boys.
Soon they were on their way to
Scrooge's mansion in Duckburg.
Launchpad was good at
flying helicopters.

But he was not so good at landing them!
"Look out!" yelled Scrooge. "You're
going to land on my house!"
"Don't worry, Mr. McD," said Launchpad.
"I don't land on houses."

Launchpad was right.
He didn't land on the house.
But he did land in Scrooge's fountain!

Huey, Dewey, and Louie looked around.
They were worried.
"What will it be like here?"
the boys wondered.
The mansion looked more like a prison
than a home!

"Remember, boys," said Scrooge.
"No touching, no playing, no running...
No anything while you are here!
This is my butler, Duckworth.
He will see to it that you
behave properly!"

"Oh, no," the boys thought.
"This place IS like a prison!"

Duckworth gave the boys
their suitcases.

Then the boys went up to their room.

The boys unpacked their toys.

"This place isn't too bad," said Louie.

"There's lots of room to play games!"

The next few days were not easy
for poor Duckworth.

He was used to serving tea.

He was not used to keeping up
with three playful boys.

One day Duckworth went to see Scrooge.
"It is not my job to look after boys, sir,"
said Duckworth.

"All right, Duckworth," said Scrooge.
Scrooge picked up the telephone.

Scrooge called a job agency.
"Send me a baby-sitter right away.
She must be used to handling wild boys!"
Scrooge hung up and said, "Don't worry,
Duckworth. Help is on the way!"

The next day Mrs. Beakley arrived.
Her young niece was with her.

"My name is Webby,"
said the little girl.
"Do you want to play?
I have my jump rope
with me."

"Jump rope?" yelled the boys.
"Jump rope is a girls' game!"

Huey, Dewey, and Louie were wild boys,
but no wilder than most little boys.
Mrs. Beakley had no trouble with them!

Mrs. Beakley soon had the boys neat,
clean, and behaving like perfect
gentlemen.

Meanwhile, on the other side of town,
there lived three bad characters
who were NOT gentlemen.

They were burglars called
the Beagle Boys!

"I'm hungry," said one Beagle Boy.
"What's for lunch?"

"Nothing," said another.
"We have no food."

"We have no money, either,"
said the third.

"What are we waiting for?"
said their leader.

"It's time we visited the mansion of
Scrooge McDuck. And we should do it
when he's not at home!"

The Beagle Boys got their tools.
They climbed into their car.

Nothing made the Beagle Boys happier
than taking things that did not belong
to them!

The Beagle Boys parked their car
near Scrooge's mansion.

Then they hid behind some bushes.

"Look," the leader whispered. "Scrooge
and his butler are leaving. As soon as
they're gone, the coast will be clear!"

The burglars chuckled as the limousine
drove away.

They did not know that five new ducks
had just moved in with Scrooge!

The burglars forced open a window.

"Come on," said the leader. "Scrooge
will be gone all day. We can fill the car
with McDuck's moneybags!"

"If we had a truck, we could take
everything in the house," said his friend.

Upstairs, Webby was in the boys' room.
"Are you going to listen to music
all day? Why don't we play?" Webby said.
"We'd rather listen to music,"
said Huey. "We can't hear you! Go away!"

"It's always the same," thought Webby.
"They won't play with me because
I'm a girl!"
   Suddenly Webby heard a strange noise.
It sounded like heavy footsteps!

The noise scared Webby.
She hid behind an old suit of armor.
The footsteps got louder and louder.
They came closer and closer!

Webby saw three shadows coming up the stairs.

"Oh, no!" thought Webby. "That's not Scrooge or Duckworth! Who can it be?"

Webby ran back to the boys' room.
"There are strangers in the house!"
Webby said.
"We can't hear you!" said the boys.

As Webby came out into the hall,
she saw the Beagle Boys leaving!

Webby thought, "Aunt Beakley is outside
and can't help. The boys can't hear and
won't help. I'll just have to stop those
burglars all by myself!"

Webby got Louie's skateboard and marbles.
She rolled them at the burglars' feet!

The Beagle Boys didn't see the marbles
and skateboard rolling toward them.
Before they knew it, they stepped
right on the toys.

"Yeeeow!" yelled the Beagle Boys.
Their feet slipped out from under them.
All three burglars crashed to the floor.
The suit of armor fell on top of them.

"That will teach you guys!" said Webby.
Webby quickly tied up the Beagle Boys
with her jump rope.

The boys' music was loud.
But the noise in the hall was louder.
Huey, Dewey, and Louie ran
out of their room.
"Gosh!" shouted Dewey. "Webby caught
the Beagle Boys!"

Just then, Scrooge came home.
Mrs. Beakley was waiting for him.
Scrooge saw a big mess and said, "Have those bad boys been making trouble again?"

"No, Mr. McDuck," said Mrs. Beakley.
"These good boys saved your house
from burglars!"

"No," said Huey. "Webby did it all
by herself. She outsmarted those crooks!"

"Well done, Webby!" said Scrooge.

The police took the Beagle Boys away.
The burglars were very embarrassed.
They had been caught by a little girl!

"You're not so bad, Webby," said Huey.
"How about playing with us?" asked Dewey.
"We could go roller skating," said Louie.
"Maybe," said Webby. "And then
we can play with my jump rope!"